DEDICATION:

TO MY ROCK ANGEL TAMARA, MY FAITH ANGELS, MY CHILDREN, JESSICAH AND MATTHEW, MY NEWEST ANGEL, GRANDSON, AYDEN,

THE ANGELIC ANCESTORS: **MARY ELLEN, JANIE MARIE, "SISTER" EDDIE B., BERTHA B., SHAUNDRA, MICHAEL, "TEDDY BEAR" G. HEARD.**

ABOUT THE AUTHOR

WILLIAM NEMON HEARD IS A SINGER, SONG WRITER, PRODUCER, AUTHOR, COUNSELOR, ORDAINED MINISTER, CHRISTIAN EDUCATOR, CONSULTANT, AND ENTREPRENEUR. HE COMPLETED STUDIES IN BUSINESS ADMINISTRATION, VOCAL PERFORMANCE, PSYCHOLOGY, DIVINITY, PASTORAL CARE AND COUNSELING, PASTORAL THEOLOGY, AND CONGREGATIONS MINISTRIES. HE IS A GRADUATE OF PRINCETON THEOLOGICAL SEMINARY – MDIV, 2004, THM 2005. WILLIAM SERVED IN MULTIFACETED CAPACITIES IN A LIFE IN THE AFRICAN AMERICAN CHURCH IN AREAS OF SACRED ARTS MINISTRIES, MEDIA, LEADERSHIP, ADMINISTRATIONS, EDUCATION, FAMILY LIFE, ORGANIZATION CREATION, PASTORAL MINISTRY. HE ALSO COLLABORATED WITH INTERDENOMINATIONAL, INTERFAITH, CIVIC, AND MENTAL HEALTH ORGANIZATIONS.

HEARD HAS WRITTEN, ARRANGED, PERFORMED, AND PRODUCED MUSIC OVER 5 DECADES. WILLIAM HAS PRODUCED A THREE VOLUME COMPILATION OF ALBUMS ENTITLED SONGS FROM THE SANCTUARY HYMNS SPIRITUALS & CLASSIC GOSPELS, AND RECENTLY RELEASED A GOSPEL MUSIC SINGLE "ONE MORE DAY" ON HIS LABEL HEARDSONG PRODUCTIONS LLC THROUGH HIS PUBLISHING COMPANY HEARD THE WORD MUSIC. BILL HAS DREAMED OF WRITING FOR CHILDREN, TEENS, AND ADULTS FOR MANY YEARS AS HE WORKED AND STUDIED. IN THE MEANTIME, HE FORMULATED STORY IDEAS, TITLES, AND OUTLINES AND NOW REALIZES THE FIRST STEPS IN THAT VISION WITH TWO INAUGURAL BOOKS IN THE "SAFE PLACES" SERIES AND AN ANIMAL ADVENTURE BOOK SERIES, "RUN-BILLY-RUN! THE ADVENTURES OF BILLY-BLUE AND HIS FRIENDS". HE CONSIDERS HIMSELF A "GRIOT", IN THE TRADITION OF THE AFRICAN STORYTELLER. THESE HISTORIC MUSICAL AND BOOK PROJECTS ARE AVAILABLE AT AMAZON, ITUNES, GOOGLEMUSIC, PANDORA AND ALL MAJOR VENUES.

ACKNOWLEDGEMENT:

THANKS TO THE "…GIVER OF EVERY GOOD AND PERFECT GIFT…" FOR THE GIFT OF STORYTELLING, THROUGH WHICH WE OVERCOME AND ARE ENCOURAGED TO PRESS/LIVE ON.

WE HONOR THE HISTORIC AFRICAN GRIOT WHO SERVED AS A REPOSITORY FOR TRIBAL HISTORY, FOLKLORE, WISDOM, AND VISION.

THANKS TO MY WIFE AND CHILDREN WHO HAVE CAJOLED ME INTO REACHING FOR AND REALIZING THE DREAM OF WRITING AND SHARING MY WISDOM, VISION, AND GIFTS.

THANKS TO ALL THE CHILDREN, YOUTH, FAMILIES, AND COMMUNITIES WHO INSPIRED THESE WRITINGS AND DEMONSTRATED A NEED FOR SUCH STORIES OF HOPE, RESILIENCE, AND RESOLVE.

THANKS TO THE VILLAGE OF ENCOURAGERS ON THE JOURNEY WHO BELIEVED, PRAYED, SHARED WISDOM, AND RESEARCH. KUDOS TO NBP STAFF FOR YOUR PROFESSIONALISM, PROJECT SUPPORT, AND CREATIVE ENERGY.

RUN BILLY RUN – RUN BILLY RUN
RUN BILLY RUN BILLY RUN BILLY RUN
SEE BILLY RUN - WATCH BILLY RUN
RUN BILLY RUN YOU CAN
REALLY REALLY RUN

BILLY RUNS IN THE RAIN
BILLY RUNS IN THE SUN

BILLY RUNS IN THE WIND
BILLY RUNS IN THE NIGHT

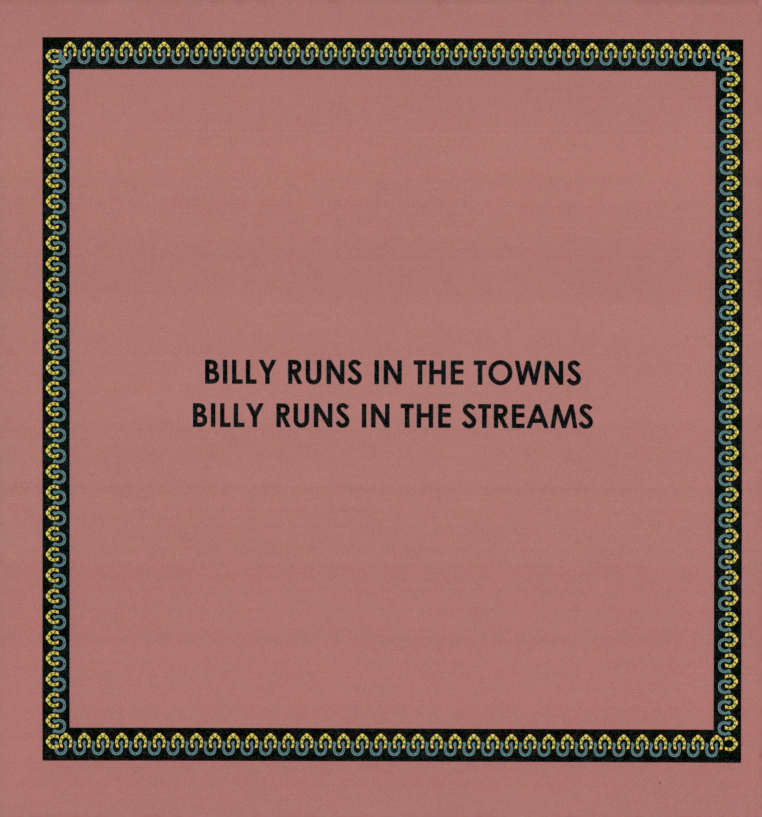

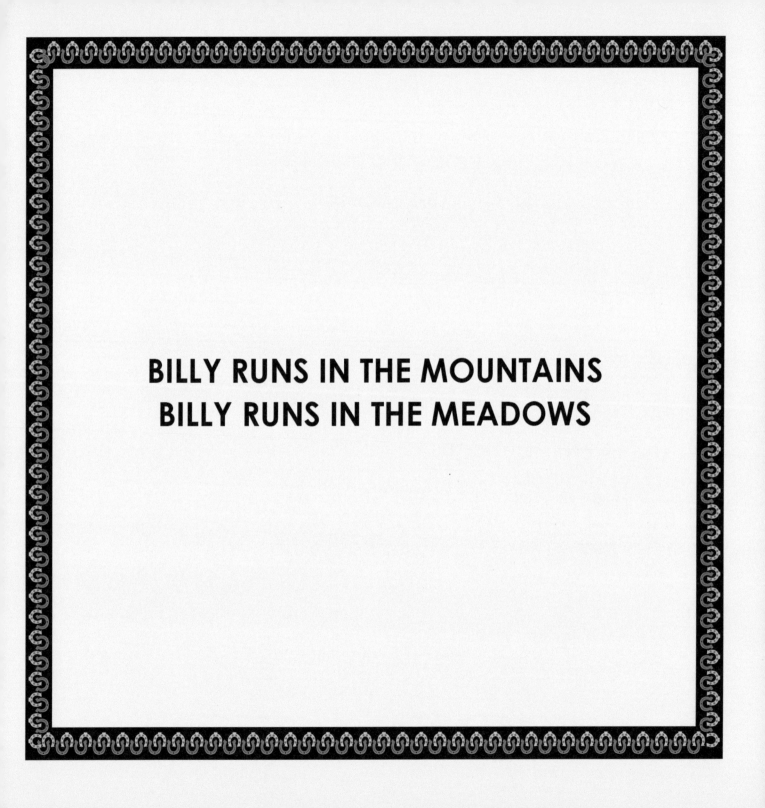

BILLY RUNS IN THE MOUNTAINS
BILLY RUNS IN THE MEADOWS

BILLY RUNS IN THE COUNTRY
BILLY RUNS IN THE CITIES

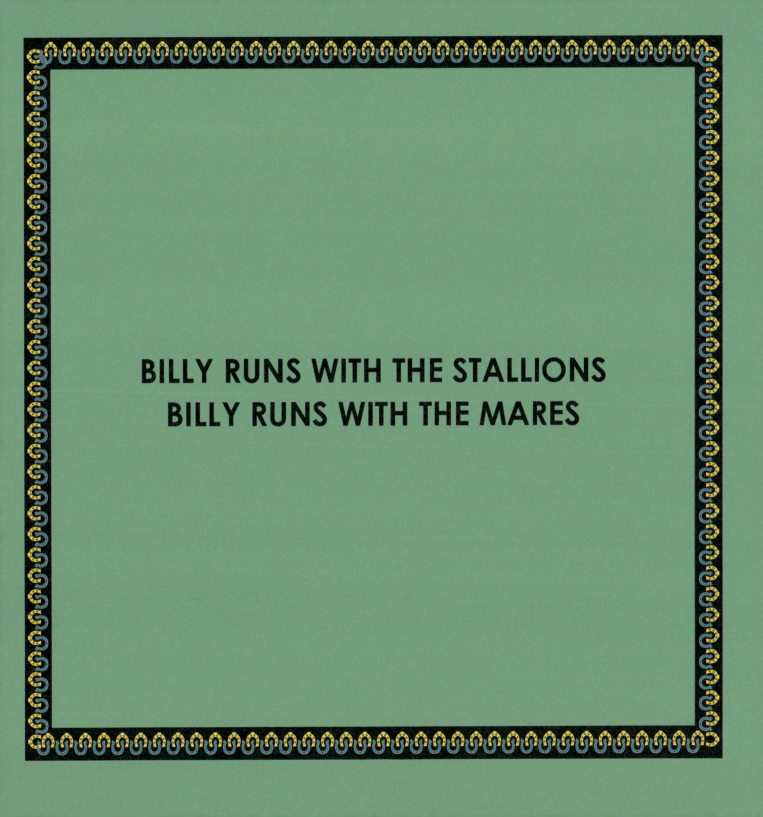

BILLY RUNS WITH THE BISON
BILLY RUNS WITH DEER

BILLY RUNS WITH THE RHINO
BILLY RUNS WITH THE GAZELLE

BILLY RUNS WITH HIS FRIENDS
BILLY RUNS WITH THE HERDS

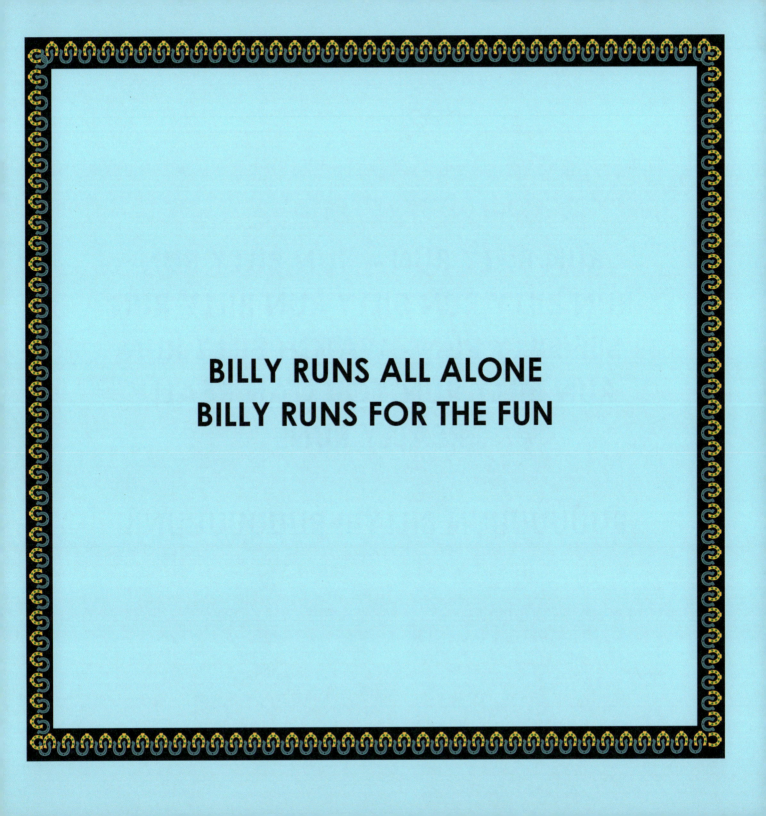

RUN BILLY RUN – RUN BILLY RUN
RUN BILLY RUN BILLY RUN BILLY RUN
SEE BILLY RUN - WATCH BILLY RUN
RUN BILLY RUN YOU CAN REALLY
REALLY RUN!

RUUUUUUUN BILLY!!! RUUUUUUUN!!!

©Copyright 2023 Golden Griot Book Publishing, All Rights Reserved

Made in United States
Troutdale, OR
01/04/2024